Logan and Lexi Meditate

Denesia D. Rodgers
Illustrations by Baba Mustapha

atmosphere press

© 2022 Denesia Rodgers

Published by Atmosphere Press

No part of this book may be reproduced without permission from the author except in brief quotations and in reviews.

atmospherepress.com

I'd like to dedicate this book to Logan and Lexi Rodgers, my two daughters, who were my inspiration for writing this story. I hope it will allow other kids to discover how yoga and meditation can help them in their lives.

May we all find alternate ways to manage stress, anxiety, and the many challenges of life.

DAD MOM

LOGAN   LEXI

It is 8:00 p.m. and time for Logan and Lexi to get ready for bed. Mommy encourages the girls to clean their dishes, kiss Daddy goodnight, and head upstairs.

Mommy noticed during dinner that Logan had a sad look on her face. She asks Logan what is wrong. Logan's eyes well up as she tells Mommy how worried she is about her final school project due in a few days. Logan is nervous about not doing well on her project.

Mommy pulls Logan aside and kneels next to her. She wipes Logan's tears and whispers, "Do you remember what we do when we are sad, worried, and down?"

Logan looks up and asks, "Meditation?"

"Yes, let's go upstairs and do some yoga and meditation to help you relax before your big school project. It will all be just fine."

Lexi blurts out, "Mommy, I want to do meditation! My day was sad, too."

Mommy smiles at Lexi and says, "Of course."

The girls head upstairs, brush their teeth, wash their faces, and go potty before bed.

Mommy, Logan, and Lexi all sit on the girls' bedroom floor. Mommy asks, "Are you girls ready for yoga and meditation?"

Logan and Lexi respond, "Yes, Mommy, we are ready."

Logan's spirits already seemed a little higher after setting her worry about the school project aside.

"Alright, girls, let's begin in child's pose. Come onto your knees, lower your bums to your heels, and release your arms out in front of you. As you get settled in your child's pose, you breathe in, and you breathe out. You breathe in, and you breathe out."

Mommy, Logan and Lexi all begin to settle into child's pose. Both girls are still as a log as they breathe easily in and out of their nose to calm their minds.

"Now, let's come into a tabletop position with your knees down, toes untucked, and your palms facing down on the floor," says Mommy.

Logan asks, "Mommy, can we do our cat and cow?"

Mommy answers, "Yes, Logan. Let's move through our cat and cow poses."

Mommy continues, "In your tabletop position, begin to lower the belly and look forward and say MOO! Then round your back like an angry cat and say MEOW!"

The girls begin to chant, "MOO! MEOW! MOO! MEOW!"

Logan and Lexi giggle as they move through their cat and cow poses. Mommy continues to see a change in Logan's mood.

"Next, let's do our downward-facing dog pose," Mommy says. "Tuck your toes, lift those hips! Now walk your dog by pedaling your feet. Then, lift one leg in the air, set it down, and then lift the other leg."

Logan and Lexi begin to walk their dog, wiggle around, and lift one leg in the air at a time.

"Girls, begin to walk your feet to your hands and stand up tall, like a very tall mountain."

Logan and Lexi hurry their feet to their hands and stand up tall with their hands by their sides. Then, Logan asks if they could do tree pose. Mommy smiles and nods.

Mommy leads the girls through one of their favorite balancing postures, tree pose.

"Begin to stand up nice and tall like a tree. Balancing on one foot, place the other foot anywhere along your standing leg."

Logan and Lexi wiggle and wobble as they balance on one foot like a tree and put the other foot on the standing leg. Lexi topples down and bursts out laughing. Logan balances on one leg and begins to grow her tree by reaching her arms over her head.

Logan says, "You breathe in, grow tall as a tree, and you breathe out, letting your leaves fall slowly. Breathe in and breathe out, allowing your tree leaves to fall."

"Okay, girls," Mommy says, "let's end our night with some meditation to get us calm and settled. Come on down to your seats and cross your legs."

Logan and Lexi sit down and cross their legs in front of Mommy.

"Allow your eyes to close and begin to relax."

Mommy closes her eyes. Logan and Lexi close theirs, too.

"Now relax your shoulders and breathe in and out of your nose."

Logan's face begins to soften. The tension in her body begins to release as she sits next to Mommy and her sister in her meditation pose.

Mommy encourages the girls to always use meditation to help them when they are worried, sad, and anxious. Meditation is an excellent way to help reduce stress, balance emotions, and feel grounded.

"Lexi, what breath do you want to do tonight?" Mommy asks.

A big smile spreads across Lexi's face. She shouts, "Baby's breath! You breathe in, and you breathe out WAAH! You breathe in, and you breathe out WAAH."

Everyone bursts out in laughter. Lexi loves to end her day with baby's breath.

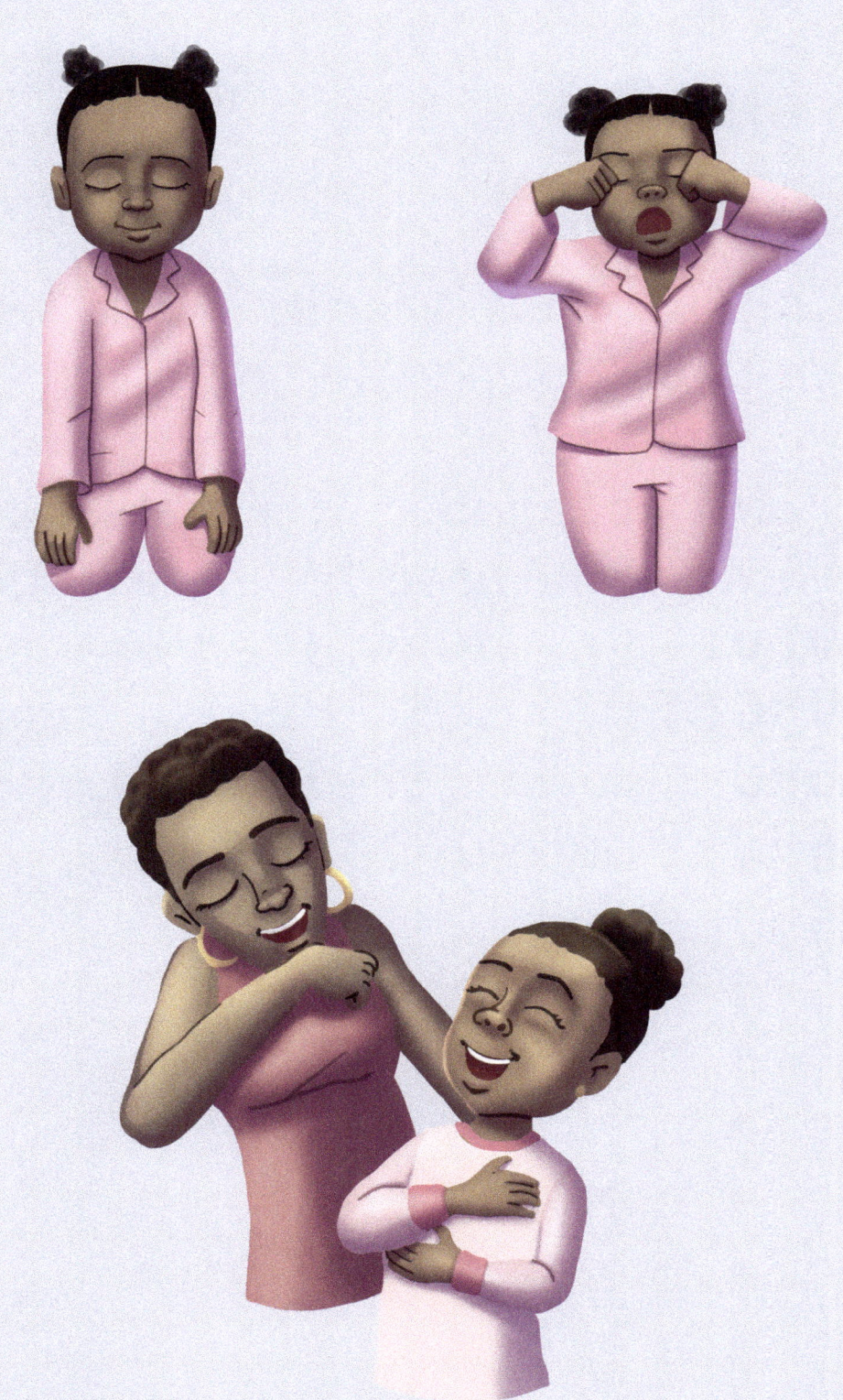

"Logan, what breath would you like to do?" asks Mommy.

Logan responds, "First, blanket breath. You breathe in, lift your hands up, and breathe out WHOOSH, and release your hands down. Breathe in and breathe out WHOOSH."

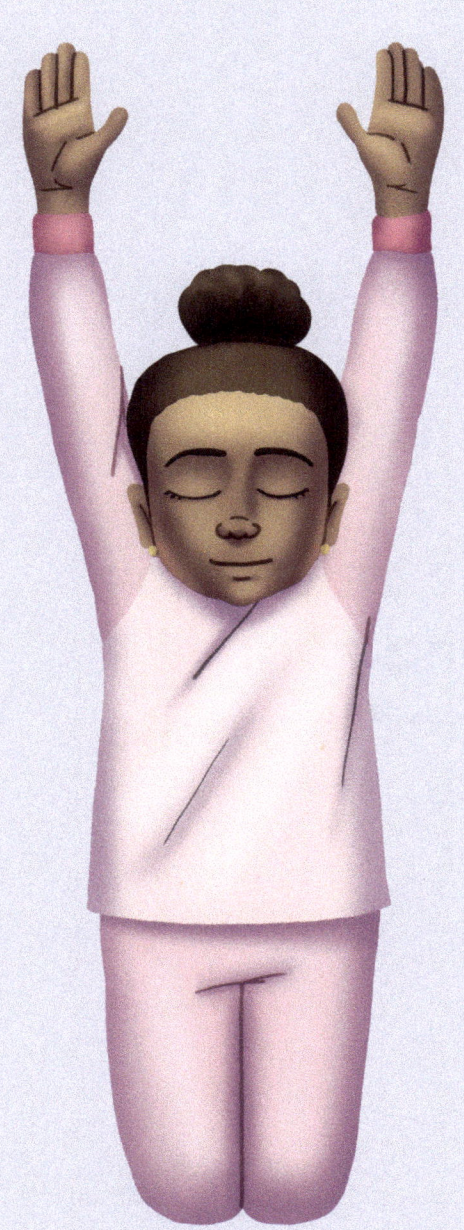

"Next," Logan continues, "Let's do lion's breath. You breathe in and you breathe out, stick out your tongue, and roar like a lion. Breathe in and breathe out, ROAR!"

The girls continue for a few more minutes, going through baby's breath, blanket breath, and lion's breath.

"Okay, girls, it's time for bed." Logan and Lexi rise slowly to make their way to their beds.

Logan notices that she is feeling calm and relaxed as she recites her prayers.

Mommy tucks the girls in.

Logan says to Mommy, "Thank you, Mommy. I am not sad anymore about my project. I feel so much better, and I know I will do great!"

"Yes, you will do fantastic," Mommy says.

She kisses Logan and Lexi before turning off the light. "Sweet dreams, baby girls."

About the Author

Yoga and Meditation teacher, mom of two, and lifelong learner. Denesia D. Rodgers was born in Port of Spain, Trinidad and Tobago, to Rev. Dr. Carol D. Parris and Vaughn R. Parris. She was raised in northern New Jersey and has three wonderful siblings (Nicole T. Smith, Jason M. Parris, and Dwayne C. Parris). Denesia found her home in Washington, DC, where she met her husband, Lionel A. Rodgers, a high school teacher, former head football coach, and DC native. She is mom to Logan A. Rodgers, Lexi A. Rodgers, her American Akita Lucas, and over 20 house plants. She holds a Bachelor of Arts in Sociology from Johns Hopkins University and a Master's in Public Health in Health Services, Management, and Policy from Tufts University School of Medicine.

Denesia's yoga journey began in 2013 when she was looking for healing and strength to combat her lifelong struggle with scoliosis. She founded Healing Power Yoga DC, her yoga brand geared towards making yoga and meditation accessible for all communities, in 2020. She firmly believes that yoga should be accessible to all regardless of age, gender, race, and physical limitations. Yoga and meditation have played a considerable part in her path to healing. Denesia's mission is to share this practice with others to help them find their own healing.

About Atmosphere Press

Atmosphere Press is an independent, full-service publisher for excellent books in all genres and for all audiences. Learn more about what we do at atmospherepress.com.

We encourage you to check out some of Atmosphere's latest releases, which are available at Amazon.com and via order from your local bookstore:

Gloppy, by Janice Laakko
Wildly Perfect, by Brooke McMahan
How Grizzly Found Gratitude, by Dennis Mathew
Do Lions Cry?, by Erina White
Sadie and Charley Finding Their Way, by Bonnie Griesemer
Silly Sam and the Invisible Jinni, by Shayla Emran Bajalia
Feeling My Feelings, by Shilpi Mahajan
Zombie Mombie Saves the Day, by Kelly Lucero
The Fable King, by Sarah Philpot
Blue Goggles for Lizzy, by Amanda Cumbey
Neville and the Adventure to Cricket Creek, by Juliana Houston
Peculiar Pets: A Collection of Exotic and Quixotic Animal Poems, by Kerry Cramer
Carlito the Bat Learns to Trick-or-Treat, by Michele Lizet Flores
Zoo Dance Party, by Joshua Mutters
Beau Wants to Know, a picture book by Brian Sullivan
The King's Drapes, a picture book by Jocelyn Tambascio
You are the Moon, a picture book by Shana Rachel Diot
Onionhead, a picture book by Gary Ziskovsky

CPSIA information can be obtained
at www.ICGtesting.com
Printed in the USA
LVHW072245100622
721008LV00001B/1